Chapter One:

The Pimp

"Bitch, I know you holding out on me! Where's my fucking money? Huh? Ungrateful ass ho!"

"I'm sorry, Daddy. I ain't mean to. I thought it was all in that bra cup. I forgot I had split it up. Here's all your money, Daddy."

"You sorry? You sorry, huh? Ain't no motherfucking sorry, you heard? Shit better not happen again! Matter fact, imma teach you a lesson. Get on your knees. Move, bitch, move!"

Jungle watched from behind the dumpster he was hiding behind as the pimp smacked his prostitute around. She was a real pretty girl. Light-skinned, tall, real hair, fat ass. He licked his lips and debated whether or not he was gonna fuck her or just let her go. What happened next made up his mind for him.

Credits

Jack$Boi: A Tale of Urban Terror is a work of fiction

inspired by Lyfe Jennings's song "Stickup Kid". It is

authored by Darrell A. King, the King Of Urban Flash

Fiction. Credit goes to KJ Publications, Inc. CEO Darrell

King and COO Elbert Jones Jr.

Jack$Boi: A Tale of Urban Terror

by Darrell A. King

The pimp pushed her onto the ground and tore her clothes with his pocket knife, threatening to stab her. She started crying, making her heavy makeup run down her face. He then proceeded to spank her, so hard her entire ass turned red. He then dropped his pants, grabbed her neck, choked her heavily, and rammed his dick inside of her.

"I'm sorry, Daddy! I'm real sorry!" she begged. Seeing this nigga raping the bitch just turned Jungle off. Like he needed to see some other brother's dick. Fuck outta here. He sprang up from his hiding spot, pulling his lucky knife out.

"Yo, pencildick! What you think you are doing, foul-ass mothafucka? You must want some sauce, eh?" Even with his Haitian drawl, Jungle sounded fierce. Something about the look in his eyes could make the illest thug run to his mama; you could tell that he had seen and done things and had no problem demonstrating his skills.

"Who the fuck you think you talking to? I know you, nigga?"

"No, but you will never forget me after today, mothafucka. Any last wishes, brotha?"

"Last wishes? Nigga, you must be trippin--" Before he could finish his sentence, Jungle had him by the neck, lucky knife pressed up against his throat. He struggled, but Jungle elbowed his balls, making him double over in pain. He clenched his jaw and stayed still.

"Now as I was saying, any last wishes, man? I want you to look at my face and remember me for the rest of eternity." Before the pimp could make any objections, Jungle slit his throat, cutting his head clean off of his shoulders. He then patted his pockets and took all the money he had. He left his insignia at the scene, a palm tree with the word Jungle on it, and turned to leave. He then noticed the hooker still kneeling on the pavement, staring at him in shock. He swaggered over to her, bent over, and whispered in her ear: "You lucky you cute, Mama. Go home and don't tell nobody what you seen." He then slapped her ass one good time and walked away from his newest crime scene.

This wasn't the first time that Jungle had killed someone. In fact, he murdered someone new every night, sometimes multiple people, except Sundays. He wasn't full-blown Christian or anything, but just in case God was real, he didn't want to completely fuck up his relationship with Him by going on killing sprees on the sacred day of the week.

He mostly killed his victims by stabbing them or slitting their throats; his lucky knife had seen a lot of action over the years. He even had a name for it: Shakita. He had been in possession of Shakita since he was eleven years old, back in Haiti. Shakita had been the weapon that was given to him by his commander in his days of being a youth soldier. He had never expected to be drafted, but one day, some troops had shown up at his door and dragged him away, while his mother and sisters had watched him leave, tears streaming down their faces.

He was the runt of the lot; even though he was eleven, he was smaller than some of eight and nine year olds. He was picked on almost incessantly and made to feel weaker than his fellow soldiers. He had been told that he would never even make it past training before he died.

This had made him determined to prove his bullies wrong. He trained harder than any of the others, and what he lacked in size, he made up for in stealth. Once in combat, he witnessed his comrades dropping like flies, one by one, while he became a stone-cold assassin. Served those cocky-ass motherfuckers right anyway.

Jungle had been like a ninja, the blackest fucking ninja ever, but still a ninja. He cut throats like it was no joke. And the sickest part was the fact that no one ever saw him coming. They never stood a chance--any of them. He had killed men, women, and other children, and a part of him didn't even care sometimes. He was becoming a savage.

Jungle was rescued from the Islamic warlord ruling his township by NATO forces about six months after he had begun training and three weeks after his first kill. In that time, he had managed to catch over fifty bodies. He sure had been one tough little kid, that's for sure.

They took him to the United States, Baltimore, Maryland to be exact, and raised him in foster care. He never saw his mama and sisters again, but he knew they were most likely dead--his village had been bombed when NATO gained control. Growing up in the system had been tough for him. He was an angry kid and got into fights with his foster brothers and sisters all the time. He had even gotten into it with a few of his caregivers. They had kept shipping him from foster home to foster home to group home to group home, so he had never really had a place to call his home.

The state had forced him to go to therapy throughout his teenage years because of his troublemaking. Not only was he aggressive at "home" but also at school. He had been caught stealing things and smoking weed on a few occasions as well, but the last straw had been when one of his foster mothers caught him stabbing a squirrel to death in their backyard. His case worker had taken him to see a doctor who had diagnosed him with Post-Traumatic Stress Disorder and sent him to a state psychologist.

Therapy had always been complete bullshit to Jungle. They wanted him to talk through his problems and "heal from the trauma he had endured". Whatever, man. They weren't there. They didn't know anything about what he had been through. Fuck the system. As he got a bit older, he came to his own realizations that he shouldn't steal or deal drugs--his mama had always told him not to go down that path. But that had left him with no outlet for all of his anger, because pretty soon, killing animals stopped giving him satisfaction. That's when shit got real, you feel me?

Chapter Two:

The Girlfriend

"Let me get two chicken boxes. Salt, pepper, ketchup

on that. Thanks, man." Kwame paid, picked up the

chicken boxes from the front counter, and walked over to Jungle. "Here, man," he said, handing Jungle one of the boxes. Jungle opened the box, inspected the wings, and tasted one of the potato wedges carefully. He placed it back down after biting it and added more salt, pepper, and ketchup, like a true Baltimorean.

"Thank you, my nigga. I got you for lunch tomorrow, ya heard?" They headed out of the chicken spot and walked back to the truck, munching on a couple fries on the way.

"Hey, Torin, think you can do a couple deliveries by yourself? Hate to do that to you but I got a coupla things I gotta take care of what with the holidays being right around the corner, you feel me? I just need to pick up some stuff for the kids from that place round the corner if you could just come back in a couple hours or so…"

Torin was Jungle's real name; the one people called him during the day when they weren't potential prey. Torin Ademyi, UPS delivery driver by day; Jungle, vicious serial killer by night.

"Yeah, no problem, brotha. I gotchu, man." Jungle dapped him up and climbed into the driver's seat of the truck, fueled on fried chicken and ready to deliver some shit to some people. He looked through the list of deliveries, smirked, and revved up the engine. This was gonna be a damn good day.

After a long route of package delivery, he wound up at the final house: the house of Janay Williams. Torin had met Janay several months ago when she had first moved to town and began ordering furnishings for her home. She was one bad ass chick and he told her so from the first day. They had been having a bit of a thing going on lately but he knew she was a bit more into him than he was into her. For real for real, the bitch was crazy about him. He liked her and everything but he wasn't about to make her his wife.

He grabbed the small package from the passenger's seat of the truck and swaggered up the front steps onto the porch. Before he could even ring the bell, she was at the door, arms crossed, watching him come closer. He tried to enter the house with her package the way he usually did, but she was barring his way in.

"Oh so now you wanna come up in my house? It's been three weeks since I seen you, my nigga. So I can only get yo ass over here by spending my hard-earned money to buy some shit through UPS? Yo, that shit is crazy! So what's up, brother? What you tryna do here, cuz I told you from the jump I ain't tryna be nobody's second priority. You ain't called me; you ain't been answering my texts. I don't even have words for you right now, nigga. I don't even know what the fuck to say for real for real."

"Shhh, bae. You know it's not like that. I just been real busy trying to make that money, ya heard? I been thinking about you every day. You know you always in my heart NayNay. I lost my phone and gotta get a new one, so I didn't get no calls or texts. I shoulda come over, I know, but I been so busy bae."

"Hmmmph. Sure it was. All that money you busy tryna make, and you couldn't buy no damn trap phone or nothing? Yeah right. You just been too busy fucking other bitches that's what it is."

Torin put the package down, reached into his pocket, and retrieved a small Tiffany box. He flipped the top open to reveal a white gold necklace laced with diamonds. "I didn't have no money for that cuz I was trying to save up the money to get you this. Your birthday was last weekend, and I didn't have nothing to give you. That made me feel like shit cuz you my baby. I was too embarrassed to show my face til I had bought you something as beautiful as you are."

Janay stood in shock for a few moments and then tenderly picked up the necklace and inspected it. She looked teary-eyed. "Awww baby! I knew you still loved me! This musta been like a thousand dollars though, babe! I can't accept this."

Torin laughed lightly. "A bit more than that actually, but who's counting? You what's important, bae. It's yours. Take it. Here, let me help you put it on." He gently spun her around, took the necklace out of her hand, moved her weave out of the way, and clasped the necklace around her smooth caramel neck.

"You look stunnin malady. But then again, you always do, even in sweatpants." He was really working his charm. What she didn't know was a couple Gs was nothing to him. He could make that in one night of "Jungle Hunting." In fact, he had. He'd gone to Tiffany's with the cash he'd taken from that pimp last night. He was really just aiming for some of that A1 pussy right now, and he had a feeling he was gonna get it too.

"Awwwwww...Baeeeeeeeeeeeee. I love you so fucking much, you know that? You a real nigga."

She walked into the house, leaving the door open behind her. Torin held the screen door open, grabbed the package from the porch, and followed her in. He threw the box on the couch and closed and bolted the front door. He scanned the house for her and spotted her in the kitchen, getting some juice. Perfect. He smiled naughtily.

In less than a second, he was behind her, pinning the refrigerator door closed with her body. He grabbed her ass and started kissing and biting her neck. Then he picked her up, laid her on the kitchen table, and pulled her dress off in one quick motion.

"Mmm, babe. You so strong." Janay was staring up at him, biting her bottom lip.

Torin put his hand over her pussy, felt how incredibly wet it was, and smiled. He was in her in a matter of seconds, thrusting hard and choking her. After a few minutes of intense fucking, he finally couldn't take it anymore and let himself bust right inside of her, claiming her with his DNA. Then he pulled the morning after pill he had bought earlier out of his pocket and watched her swallow it. *Good girl*, he thought.

A few minutes later, Torin was lounging on the couch watching a game. Janay walked over and sat a bowl of ice cream and cookies on the coffee table in front of him. Man, he had her whipped. Fuckin' A.

"Hey, did you hear about that Jungle killing last night? This time it was some pimp he fucked up." Torin looked at her, seemingly in surprise, so she kept talking. "Yeah, I know. This nigga crazy as fuck. That's like twenty bodies this year so far. All the dope boys and

pimps and everybody really scared as fuck. Be careful

babe, aight? I don't want nothin happenin to you."

Chapter Three:

The Prison Guard

Later that night, Torin thought about what Janay had said while he was getting ready for his second job. Torin also worked for a local janitorial company, during the night, more for cover than anything else. If he stepped out to hunt, no one would even realize he was gone, and if the cops ever suspected him, he had an automatic alibi.

Jungle was gaining a lot of credit, and it was really making him proud. East Baltimore was no joke. There were real criminals up in this bitch, and they were all scared of him. He laughed, imagining what they would think if they ever found out that Jungle the serial killer was really a twenty-two year old Haitian UPS driver/janitor. Just thinking about it cracked him up.

Torin got into his black sedan, which also doubled as his Jungle mobile when he took the license plates off, and GPSed the job location his boss had given him earlier. He was working a new place tonight--a prison facility, ironically. It sure was gonna be fun to "break out" of jail and go kill people right under the cops' noses.

After about twenty minutes of driving, Torin pulled up in front of the building, pulled out his cleaning supplies, and made sure that his killing supplies were well-hidden in the trunk. Then, he smoothly walked over to check-in so that he could begin his job.

After check-in, he was greeted by a corrections officer by the name of Dontae Mills. Surprisingly, he appeared to be the chief officer at the prison, even though he was black. He seemed to be a pretty cool dude. Usually people just barked orders at him when he cleaned for them. Dontae actually talked to him like a fellow human being.

As Torin went from location to location, cleaning, Dontae tagged along and continued to make conversation with him. He'd never had such a chattery client before. It wasn't that annoying, though. It was actually nice to have some company for a change.

The only annoying part was that he wasn't sure how he was going to disappear to do his hunting later. He might have to wait until the job was over, and then he wouldn't have an alibi for the night, which sucked dicked, to say the least. At least he was good at not getting caught, on everything, or else he might've had a problem.

While he was mopping up one of the unoccupied cells, Dontae started talking about the Freddy Gray death and how it had been affecting the community, with a behind the scenes kind of look at it from the Baltimore law enforcement community. Jungle had been contemplating taking out some dirty cops since the death and ensuing riots but wasn't sure where to start.

It was easy to spot the drug dealers standing on the corners in their foamposites or the pimps and prostitutes; it was pretty damn hard, however, to figure out which cops were racist son-of-bitches and which were genuinely concerned about keeping the community safe. The last thing he needed was to take out some of the good cops as well and leave his hood even more dangerous.

"Keep this on the DL, Torin, but it's some pretty fucked up shit going on here in the Baltimore PD. As a devout police officer and black male, I am honestly appalled by the almost gang-like activities going on in the police department." Dontae looked almost mystified, as if what activities he was thinking about were still shocking to him.

"Yeah, man, I won't say a word to nobody. You my nigga now, and whatever you say to me is between us."

Torin lowered his voice before continuing. "What's been going on that got you so freaked out, brotha?"

Dontae looked around and lowered his voice conspiratorially as well. "Well, word in the department is that there's this "gang" of dirty cops floating around, targeting young black males. They've been keeping it on the hush-hush, if you know what I'm saying, but there's been victims as young as twelve, ranging to the oldest so far, who was thirty. Most of the victims have been in their early twenties, though, around twenty-two or twenty-three. There's also been a few rapes of young black females, but I think the department has been paying them off not to say anything, which is pretty fucked up."

"Damn." That's all Torin could say. All of his shock, hatred, disgust, and grief for his community was all reflected in that one word.

"I know. This is one fucked up world we live in now, that's for sure, Torin. What's even worse is that I think there's a few black cops involved in the gang as well. I'll never understand the need of some well-brought-up African American men to kiss the asses of the whites.

Those motherfuckers should be kissing our asses instead of raping our daughters and killing our sons. I went to the Police Academy so that I could actually make a difference in the world. Help clean up the streets of my hood. Now I find out they're being dirtied by people who are supposed to be 'my brothers?' That shit's crazy."

"What do these dirty cops call their lil nigger-killing gang?"

"The Dawg Catcherz."

Chapter Four:

The Night

Torin barely got any sleep after leaving the prison. He was so out of it, he didn't even feel like hunting that night. He created Jungle to satiate his bloodthirst while being on that paperchase at the same damn time. But, suddenly, he wanted to use Jungle for something else…something more meaningful to the community than taking out a few dope dealers.

Dontae had really given him something to think about, and thinking is exactly what he did. Dontae had went on to tell him that the rogue cops usually hunted their prey after nightfall--the same time that Jungle usually left his mark. Yes, Dontae had mentioned Jungle as well. But he didn't seem to think that Jungle was as dangerous as the Dawg Catcherz.

In fact, Dontae had even commented that Jungle was helping to rid the streets of some violent offenders that the police department was too busy to take care of. This was in reference to the fact that he had taken out a serial child rapist a few weeks back that had gotten away with his crimes.

Torin knew that he had to do something about these "nigger catchers." He couldn't just let them terrorize his community, killing his brothers and raping his sisters. The description of targets that Dontae had given fit so many of the people that Torin was closest to.

He couldn't help thinking that they might catch him in his nightly acts and execute him rather than arrest him. Or, one of them might rape Janay and get her pregnant. The only baby that Janay was going to have would be his if he ever decided he wanted kids.

Sure, he acted like he didn't really care about her sometimes, but, truthfully, he did care. She was beautiful, intelligent, and strong. She was the only woman that ever talked back to him, and he did admire her a lot. Plus, the sex was amazing. He just wasn't ready for commitment and knew that she would leave the second he revealed his true self to her.

Anyway, he knew he couldn't stand back and just let this shit happen. This was his hood. The only one allowed to prey on and kill people in these streets was Jungle.

He decided that he was going to start taking care of these ignorant fools the very next night. After coming to this conclusion and formulating a few plots in his head, he was finally able to sleep for a few hours. Luckily, it was Saturday, and UPS didn't deliver on the weekends, so he was able to sleep in a bit in preparation for his big night.

When he woke up, he decided to pay a visit to Janay and take her out to dinner. Just in case he got caught up in some shit later and didn't make it out alive. When he pulled up to the house, Janay seemed surprised to see him.

"Didn't I just see you yesterday? You sure you at the right house, Torin?"

"Haha. Very funny, love. Just get your shoes on and get in the car. I'm taking you out to dinner."

"Really? What's the occasion?"

"Me having such a beautiful girlfriend."

"Man, you must really want some pussy, huh? Gimme a minute to get ready."

Torin chuckled behind her back as she went back in the house. She was so bold even though she was so tiny; like a little feisty chihuahua. He smiled just a bit as he sat back in the driver's seat and began playing with the radio, prepared for the long wait that was to come-- whenever a girl says gimme a minute to get ready, it means gimme an hour to pick out an outfit, shower, and do my hair and makeup.

Approximately forty-seven minutes later, Janay emerged from the house and walked over to the sedan. She looked fine as hell. She had her hair in a fancy updo and her makeup was on point. She was dressed in a sexy, tight red dress and matching heels, with bangles going up and down her arms.

When she sat next to him in the car, he couldn't help but stare at her exposed chest. Her Cs looked like DDs in that dress, and he was thanking every God known to man for blessing him with a hot body like that. He grabbed her breasts, kissed her, and revved the engine at the same time.

He decided to go all out and take her to the fanciest restaurant in town. Tonight was not a night for Boston Market. He wanted to treat her to some lobster, crab puffs, and high class dessert--some baked Alaska or some shit. He was feeling pretty damn generous for no apparent reason.

Once they were seated, Torin told Janay to order whatever she wanted, no matter the price. The typical high class girl in movies would order a salad and shit if her boyfriend said that, but Torin knew better than to expect that from Janay. Hood girls ate their asses off, *especially* if the bill was being footed by someone else.

Janay did not disappoint him. After making sure he really had enough money, she went ham on the menu.

She ordered filet mignon, shrimp vodka penne, and Chardonnay. He then added lobsters and crab legs to seal the deal.

While they were eating, Janay started opening up to him and talking about her interests and experiences. They had never really had a long conversation before. They just had sex and chatted about whatever show was on tv.

It turned out that Janay was really into photography and art and wanted to incorporate that into her life, moving forward. She had a lot of ambitions and goals and was determined to be able to make it out of the hood someday. Torin had never suspected these aspirations, and they made her stand out even more in his eyes.

Maybe this was someone he could be with officially for

awhile.

Chapter Five:

The Stakeout

Jungle sat in the front seat of his sedan with all of the lights off. He was dressed in head to toe black and could not be seen by anyone from the outside. The average person wouldn't have been able to discern anything from that position in the sedan in the pitch black, either, but Jungle's eyes had become accustomed to the dark over the years, and he could easily see everything that was going on.

Jungle had very strategically thought about the spot he was going to stakeout. He had chosen a remote spot by the piers where a lot of young black adults hung out. It was typical to find black couples or groups of friends between the ages of sixteen and twenty-five. It was busiest around ten at night typically, with only a handful of young adults hanging out by the water after midnight.

According to Dontae, the Dawg Catcherz had already hit a few spots nearby that were similar to this one. He had a gut instinct that they would strike here next. He couldn't explain it; it was like when he was fighting back in Haiti and always knew where the enemy would be hiding. He could just feel it in his bones.

Certain that he would find these rogue cops and catch them in the middle of their dastardly deeds, he positioned himself where he'd be able to see any possible action that might occur from any possible angle. He scanned his surroundings like a hawk and prepared himself for a long wait, silently munching on Dunkin Donuts to keep his energy up.

By twelve-thirty, the piers had mostly cleared out. There was a young man of about nineteen years sitting on one of the benches and a young couple who appeared to be in their early twenties looking out at the water at the other side of the piers. Other than them; himself; and the ducks, the place was deserted.

A little after one o'clock in the morning, Jungle heard a slight sound coming from his right. He swiveled his head in time to see a group of four cops dressed in their Baltimore PD uniforms approaching the couple that was now making out by the water. On their way to the lovebirds, they noticed the lone young man, and two of them branched off in that direction.

Jungle watched both scenes popping off at the same time. On one side, two of the Dawg Catcherz were approaching the young man, pointing their guns, and telling him to get on the ground. When he complied, they handcuffed him. On the other side, the other two cops were harassing the young couple and spewing racist slurs.

After the lone young man was handcuffed, the policemen that had captured him brought him over to the other group and sat him down next to the couple. He looked pretty shaken up, and upon closer look, Jungle saw that he was probably only seventeen rather than the initial nineteen he had thought. He was a little on the short side, with a flat top, something that had been out of style since the nineties. Jungle could tell that this kid was his own person, and he admired him for that.

The couple also appeared to be a bit frightened. The man, a six-foot-something, muscular brother was trying to put on a tough-guy front to impress his girl, but Jungle could tell that he was just as scared as the younger boy. Shit, he would've been too if he wasn't a trained assassin.

The girl was freaking out, to say the least. She was a pretty delicate-looking lady, almost like a flower, and Jungle could tell that she was fairly innocent. She was dressed modestly in loose jeans and a varsity jacket, whereas many of the hood girls here liked to wear crop tops and super tight jeans. It angered him to watch these old men scope her out like she was a piece of meat.

The Dawg Catcherz present all looked pretty similar ironically--almost as if they were clones of each other. They were all white men in their late thirties-late forties, with greying and balding hair and receding hairlines. They were wearing identical uniforms, had some degree of pot-bellyness, and had their facial hair trimmed in a similar fashion. Looking at them reminded Jungle of some sort of cult, some Ku Klux Klan shit.

Jungle inspected them closely and was able to see their name tags when he squinted his eyes: Officers Barry Langmore, Terrence Jacobs, Phillip Knight, and

Carson Perry. He flipped his car camera on and let the video roll as he had planned out. Then, he grabbed his lucky knife and got out of the car.

Chapter Six:

The Fight

The officers had their backs turned to him, so they couldn't see him coming. Their victims, however, could, and he could see the girl's eyes widening in surprise.

"Oh, look at that guys! Girlie here can't take the intensity emanating from us real men. Bet you she's never bedded someone as good as us. Just these nigger hoodlums." Carson proclaimed, tilting the girl's chin up so that she could look him in the eyes.

The girl's boyfriend got enraged when he witnessed this and tried to headbutt Carson over. "Yo, don't you go touching my girl, asswipes."

Terrence kicked him down--hard. So hard, in fact, that Jungle could hear the force of the impact. His buddies laughed and held the kid down, while Carson lifted the girl to her feet.

She and the boys continued to watch Jungle's movements, so he put his finger to his lips, signaling for them to stay quiet and not give them away. Then he pulled out his knife, grabbed Terrence by the throat, and backed away from the group by a few feet.

"Hey, Carson! Let the girl go before I slice your partna's throat."

Carson and the others looked at him in disbelief, probably wondering who this ski mask clad kid thought he was. "Oh, really? How about I kill your friends if you slice Terrence's throat?"

"What friends? I ride solo. I don't know these people, but they look like nice kids, so I would prefer if you'd leave them alone. But, if you don't, then whateva man. Imma still kill your partna and then imma come for you easily."

Jungle gave him a sickening look that he could see rattled him immensely. He watched as Carson gulped and released the girl.

"Good boy. Now, who exactly do you think you racist mothafuckas are?"

"Hey, watch your mouth boy. We're doing the town a favor. All you little niggers just roaming around here bringing crime…"

Jungle slit Terrence's throat before he could get the rest of the words out of his mouth and reached for Barry in the same instant, positioning Shakita in the proper place for maximum killing. Everyone collectively gasped in shock as Terrence's neck spewed out large amounts of blood, while he coughed up on it to his death just moments later.

"Now, you listen and you listen to me good, you good for nothin sons of bitches. Imma kill all of you eitha way. But you can go the easy way or you can go the hard way and suffa at your last moment." He pulled out Barry's gun and pointed it Phillip, while using his elbow to still hold Barry in place.

"Wha-what do you want?" Phillip asked, obviously the meekest of the bunch.

"I wanna know who the fuck this group is, what you aim to do, and who the fuck started the damn thing."

"We're not telling you a damn thing, fucking ungrateful ass nigger!" This was, as to be expected, Carson. Jungle took care of him with one precise shot to the temple and then aimed the revolver back at Phillip.

"I'm thinking I might wanna cut your dicks off for being rapists. Then imma use Shakita here to torture ya'll. Unless you wanna answer my questions. Then, I might just consider letting ya'll go back to ya'll families."

"Okay, okay. We'll answer your questions. Just please let me go." Barry pleaded.

Jungle considered it for a second and commanded Phillip to unhandcuff the three young adults they had been planning to fuck with. He then had them handcuff the two officers for payback.

"Who are you?" The girl asked him.

"I'm Jungle."

"*The* Jungle? You the one that been killing all them drug dealers and other people on the street and stealing they money?"

"Yeah. But don't worry. I'm not gonna hurt you. I only came to fuck up the dirty cops that been targeting our people. Ya'll are free to go. Hurry home and be aware of your surroundings. There's more of these fuckas out here."

The group heeded his warning and dipped as fast as they could. They probably were still scared that Jungle was gonna stick them up. He must've really been giving off a bad impression on people, if these kids were so scared that he was gonna kill them after he took the time to save them. They should've known by his pattern of killing that he wasn't gonna hurt them. He usually stuck to criminals--not kids.

Disregarding his thoughts for the moment, Jungle turned back to the dirty cops he had to deal with. Phillip was shivering, funnily enough.

"*You're* Jungle??"

"That's what the fuck I just said, ain't it, brotha?"

"But, you're just a kid! How could you possibly be behind all of these street killings??"

"You just watched me kill your two buddies, didn't you? Now shut the fuck up with the stupid questions and answer the questions I just asked you. Otherwise, imma make both of ya'll suffer."

"Wha-what was the question again, sir? I'm sorry, my brain isn't working right." Phillip was such a fucking pussy. That much was obvious.

"My questions were who the fuck are ya'll, why the fuck are ya'll doing this shit, and who the fuck decided to make this gang in the first place?"

"We're the Dawg Catcherz, like you said earlier. Our motto is, "Catch the dawgs to clean the streets.""

"How sweet. Why the fuck ya'll think we black folk is the ones dirtying the street. Ya'll descendants of the Ku Klux Klan or some crazy shit like that?"

"Oh, we're not racists! Far from it!"

"Far from it? Nigga, what the fuck you mean far from it? Ya'll targeting, raping, and killing black people. How is that not racist? Ya'll killing white people too that I don't know about or somethin cuz that statement was just fucking stupid."

"No. But we're not targeting all black people. We have nothing against the African American race. In fact, my son is married to an African American woman. She is absolutely delightful, well-mannered, polite, and lady-like, unlike some of the women you find here on the streets."

"If you don't have anything against black people, then why are you killing us?"

"We're not killing all of you. Just the hoodlums that are up to no good. Our founder made us realize that some of the black youth, the kind that are out on the street at all times of night and causing trouble need to be taken care of so that our neighborhood can be clean again and we won't have so much crime. We have nothing against the black race. In fact, our founder himself is black."

"Oh really? And who the fuck is your founder?"

"A corrections officer down at the prison. Dontae Mills."

Chapter Seven:

The Bonding

Torin's head was spinning that night as he lay in bed. It took every fiber of his being to hold himself back from speeding over to the prison and ending Dontae for good. He just couldn't believe that after everything that had happened the other night that Dontae could be the mastermind behind this whole thing.

If there was one thing Torin hated it was fakeness. He liked people to keep it real with him. They didn't have to like him and be buddy-buddy with him, but they should at least be honest with him. That's all he asked of anyone. He kept it real and liked people to keep it real with him.

He felt personally betrayed by Dontae, in a sense. Dontae had seemed so genuine when he was talking to. Someone who he could actually befriend and talk to about things in the future. And all that shit he was spitting about how sick it made him was all lies. He just wanted to brag to someone about his gang, and that was pretty fucking shitty to state the facts.

He just couldn't wrap his head around the whole scenario. How could a black man just go rogue like that against the youth of his own race. Wasn't he once a black youth? What about his brothers, uncles, father, sons, and nephews? Weren't they all previously or eventually gonna be black youth? It just made no type of sense to him.

He couldn't sleep and he didn't have work in the morning, so he decided to go for a drive. Without really thinking about where he was going, he just gassed the car and drove. Before long, he was parked in Janay's driveway. He looked around in puzzlement and asked himself why he decided to come here, but he had no answers.

He figured he might as well see if Janay was up since he was already there, so he got out of the sedan and walked up her front porch steps, cringing at the creaking and thinking to himself that he needed to fix those for her before they broke one day and she ended up hurt.

When he got to the porch, he could see through the front window that the living room lamp was on. He tapped gently on the window, and Janay appeared in the window, peering out cautiously. When she saw Torin, she looked even more shocked than she had when he had come to pick her up for dinner earlier that evening.

In a few seconds, he heard the unbolting of the front door and saw her extending the screen door open for him. He followed her inside and shut the door gently behind him.

"Are you here for a booty call Mr. Torin? If so, I hate to disappoint you, but I got my period a few hours ago and have been having some real bad cramps, so we gon have to reschedule or somethin honey."

Once again, her bluntness caught him off guard and he didn't quite know what to say. Janay sure was a different kind of lady than he was used to, and he was pretty sure that that was a good thing.

"Nah, babe, that's not why I'm here. Actually, I'm not even in the mood for sex for once," he confessed.

"Not in the mood for sex? You okay? You coming down with somethin?" She put her hands on her hips and stared at Torin as if she was worried he was about to drop dead at any second.

"Nah, I'm okay. At least, physically I am. I just--I don't know. Never mind. You wouldn't understand anyway."

"I can understand a lot more than you think I can Torin. I may be strong and bold and independent and bad as fuck on the outside, but that's only because I been through some shit my damn self."

"Like what?"

"Like being left by my birth father for his crackhead girlfriend and her kids. Being molested by my stepfather when I was five until I was ten. My mama not believing me and beating me when I told her. Getting moved around from house to house and school to school my whole life, because we was broke as fuck and kept gettin evicted. My mama sellin all the shit I owned and kickin me out when I was sixteen cuz I was taking up too much money and food and space.

Bein out on the street and havin to sell drugs and sleep with strangers just so I would have a place to stay and food to eat for the night, then havin to do it all over again the next day. Havin my heart broken time and time again cuz I was young and stupid enough to think that those niggas could love me. I been through a lot, Torin. Now what have you been through, cuz the moment I met you I saw in your eyes that you were hurtin too."

Torin let that sink in for a few moments. He had never seen Janay in a vulnerable state before. He wouldn't have thought in his wildest dreams that she would have been through all that shit in her young lifetime. Only twenty years old knowing all that pain. Life was fucking crazy. That he knew for absolute certain.

He was surprised that she was sharing all of this with him all of the sudden. Could she really sense how deeply he was hurting inside? He tried so hard his whole life to be the tough guy, the one that no one tried to mess with. He tried so hard to forget about everything that had ever happened in his life and move forward. He didn't ever want anyone to see him vulnerable and hurting.

Something inside of him was burning to confess everything to her right then and there. He had never felt so intensely about it before. After years of professional therapy, he had never once been tempted to talk about anything that had to do with his feelings, and now he just couldn't stop thinking about it.

She began stroking his hair and scratching his head, which made him feel even calmer. This woman must be a fucking witch, because he could feel himself falling under her spell.

One last kiss was all it took to make him break.

"I killed them!" he burst out.

"Woah, woah, woah, slow down. Whatcha talkin bout, babe? Explain from the beginning."

And that is exactly what he did. He told her everything, starting from the very beginning. He told her about his young life in Haiti, about his mother and his sisters. He told her about the men that had come for him one day, and he told her about the training and the vicious comments he faced from the other boys.

He told her about how hard he worked to prove everyone wrong. He told her about Shakita and how many men he had stealthily killed with her in combat. He told her about being rescued from that life and brought to the United States while his village was bombed, most likely killing his family.

He began crying for the first time in ten years when he told her about the nightmares he'd been having every night since. He told her about the struggles of growing up in the system and never having anything he wanted-- sometimes even going without the things he needed-- which was something she could relate to. Finally, he told her about his alto-ego, Jungle, and the shit that he had been doing, ending with his run-in with the Dawg Catcherz and the shocking revelation about Dontae.

Janay didn't speak a word throughout all of these confessions. She sat silently and listened, rubbing his back and wiping his tears. Even after he told her he was a serial killer, she didn't back away from him in fear the way he had initially expected her to.

"First of all, let's leak the tape. As long as it isn't obvious that it's you, we'll be okay. Most likely Dontae and those other two cops in the video will get arrested for the shit they did. Then there will be no more Dawg Catcherz cuz they won't have a leader.

Second, you can't be doing that no more. Torin, I know you are a good man. You just hurtin, just like me. We can make each other stronger, though. But you gotta stop killing people. It's not right. I know they are bad guys you trying to take out, but two wrongs don't make a right, love.

You seen a lot of shit from a young age, and that's what's causing you to feel that bloodlust. You feel angry cuz of all that shit you been through, and rightfully so, honey. You need to take your life back, but not like this. Please promise me you won't go after Dontae. It's dangerous, and it's not worth it."

They fell asleep cuddling on the couch, thoughts of what had happened finally leaving Torin's mind.

Chapter Eight:

The Confrontation

When Torin woke up, he saw that Janay had already left for work--she volunteered at a local church on Sundays. He was astonished that after confessing to being a killer last night, she had fallen asleep with him and then left him alone in her house. This definitely was one crazy girl.

Torin knew that Janay didn't want him going after Dontae, but he really saw no other solution. The cops weren't going to arrest their own based on something in a video with no source. It just wasn't what they did. He knew that he had to take things into his own hands and right his wrongs…be an actual hero.

He locked the door behind him when he left and drove over to the prison. He waited for Dontae to pull up for his shift and stopped him when he did.

"Torin! My man! You scheduled for another cleaning?"

"Nah, man. I'm here for a more personal matter."

Dontae looked a bit perplexed and waited for Torin to finish telling him the problem. "You lied to me. And I don't like liars. I also don't like dirty cops who go around killin black kids and thinkin it's okay."

"It was you last night, wasn't it? You're Jungle? No fuckin way man."

"Yes, I am."

"Well, well, well. You got some fucking nerve man. You kill two of my best men and then come back here to harass me the next day?"

Before Torin knew what was coming to him, Dontae had chloroform over his nose and was stuffing him in the backseat of his car.

When he came to, he was in the basement of what appeared to be Dontae's house, tied to a chair. Dontae was hovering over him with his gun, waiting for him to wake up.

"What you want, man? Why you doin all this crazy stuff?" Torin asked.

"I could ask you the same thing, *Jungle*."

"Why you killing your brothers and raping your sisters man? We all done come from the same place."

"Those hoodlums in the street are ruining everything for our city. All these gangs, pimps, and dopeboys. They need to be cleaned out of the street."

"What makes you think that?"

"My brother died because of them. When he was *thirteen*. He died because he was walking to the Chinese food place and got caught in the middle of a gang shoot-out. All young black kids. Just shooting up the block in the middle of the day. He had his whole fucking life ahead of him, and they took that from him. Just like they are still taking the lives of other kids, either killing them, pimping them out, or turning them to the street. It needs to be fixed, so I'm fixing it."

"Every black teen or young adult out there isn't a hoodlum that's doing bad things. What about the innocent ones? Your guys almost killed three of them last night. I think that needs to be fixed."

"Yeah, well, I think you need to be fixed."

"Oh yeah? And why's that? I didn't realize that I was broke."

"Well, I can't have you outing me before I finish my work cleaning up the streets, man. I gotta watch my back, you feel me? I'm a corrections officer. I know what the fuck goes on in jail, you feel me? I don't like what happens to be prisoners, you feel me? And I don't wanna go to jail and be a fucking prisoner, you feel me?" With every sentence, he raised the gun closer to Torin's head.

"Yeah, yeah, I feel you, man, I feel you. Let's not do anything crazy here, okay? Just take a breath and let's talk this through, aight man? I don't want no beef, ya heard?"

"If you don't want no beef, then don't mess with the cow."

"What? What cow?"

"I don't know man! I was just trying to make a cool reference, aight? Point is, you dying now. Goodbye!"

Torin braced himself for the impact as Dontae pulled the trigger. There was a shot and then nothing.

Chapter Nine:

The Resurrection

When Torin woke up, he was in the hospital and Janay was sitting at his bedside. He tried to sit up but immediately laid back down, groaning in pain.

"Don't move, baby. You got shot in the head, so everything you do is gonna hurt a bit for awhile."

"How did I get here? Where's Dontae? Why I'm not dead?"

"A part of me--a big part--knew that you would go after Dontae even though I told you not to. So, instead of going to the church, I decided to go the precinct and turn in that video that you left in your car. I told them that you had witnessed it from your car and knew Dontae personally, so you had went to go ask him if it was true.

We rushed over to the prison to stop you, but the front desk said that he was late for his shift. They went to his house to check next and heard a shot being fired when they pulled out front.

They ran down into the basement and saw you sitting there tied up, with Dontae standing over you, preparing to shoot again. They took him down and rushed you here in the ambulance. Don't worry. The rest of the Dog Catcherz squealed like rats when they heard about everything. Dontae and his friends are going away for a real long time, all cuz of that tape. You're a hero, babe."

She kissed him lightly on the lips and patted his arm. After a few seconds she became fuzzy again, and he faded back out of consciousness as the morphine kicked in.

When he woke up again, there were cops outside of the door to his hospital suite.

"Don't worry, babe, they don't know anything about you being Jungle. Just tell them that you were sitting in your car, and you'll be fine. Everything's gonna be okay."

Torin thought about that and decided that enough was enough. He needed to cleanse himself of his demons, and he needed to do it the right way.

When the officers came in to question him, he told them everything that he had told Janay, except with less emotion and detail. He confessed to being the infamous Jungle and taking out traumas from his youth out on other people by going on nightly killing and armed robbery sprees. He told them how everything with Dontae and his rogue cop buddies had really went down. He told them every terrible thing he had done, while Janay sat there crying.

When he was done confessing, they handcuffed him to his hospital bed and escorted the heartbroken Janay out of the room. He would be arraigned after the hospital cleared him to be released.

That happened a few days later. After signing his papers, two detectives escorted him in handcuffs out of the hospital and into their squad car. They then took him to the precinct to meet with the District Attorney that would be prosecuting him.

The DA offered him a deal right off the bat, as the psychiatrist from the hospital had diagnosed him with severe Post-Traumatic Stress Disorder and deemed him not completely responsible for his actions. The DA offered him one year in jail and then four years of probation after. He took the deal, and he was immediately taken in for booking.

Chapter Ten:

The Proposal

Torin couldn't help smiling on the day that he was released from jail. Most of the thugs in there were afraid of his killer reputation, so he hadn't really been bothered by anyone. He had been receiving weekly visitations from Janay, and he was really starting to develop a bond with her.

He wasn't due home until tomorrow, but they had sprung him a little early. He was hoping to surprise his lady. He made a few stops on his way to her house, then rang her doorbell.

She opened the door and was so excited she jumped up to hug him. He caught her in his arms and held her tight.

"Torin! What you doing here, boy? You wasn't supposed to get out til tomorrow!"

"I know, but I had to convince them to let me home early so that I could surprise my lovely lady."

"Man am I happy to see you! Come in!"

He followed her inside and closed the door behind him, just like old times. It felt almost as if he had never left. He looked around the living room and noticed a lot of pictures and artwork all over the walls.

Janay noticed him admiring the art. "That's some of my artwork and photography," she admitted proudly.

"Wow that looks amazing, NayNay. I'm real proud of you, chasing your dreams like that. Real proud, baby."

"Aww thank you boo. I try." She tried to sound fierce, but Torin could tell that she was slightly embarrassed. In fact, if she had been white, he was positive that she would have been blushing.

"So how have things been over here? Nobody been hitting on you without me around, have they? Cuz imma have to kill them!"

She looked so shocked at the mention of killing that he bust out laughing on the spot and couldn't even keep a straight face.

"I'm kidding, babe. No more killing for me, I swear."

"You sure about that?"

"Yeah. The therapist they hooked me up with was pretty dope. It was easy to talk to her and she really helped me out. That whole atmosphere really helped actually. It was like a break for my mind to rehabilitate and shit.

I had a nice, structured routine; meals brought to me every day; free tv…man I should ask if I can go back."

Janay slapped him playfully on the arm. "Shut up, boy. You better not be goin back to jail. I missed your monkey ass."

"Awww. Not as much as I missed you, baby. I couldn't stop thinkin bout you the whole time I was locked up in there. From the minute I woke up til I laid my head on that lumpy pillow, all I thought about was you baby girl."

He kissed her forehead and pulled her close, happy that he could finally touch her instead of looking at her through a glass divider.

"Maybe you so eager to go back cuz you found a lil man-crush up in there. You ain't dropped the soap, did you?"

"Yeah, right. I wish a nigga would try to do me like that. I would punch that mothafucka so hard he end up in France speaking Japanese. Fuck outta here!"

Janay bust out laughing and fell out onto the couch, tears of laughter rolling down her cheeks. Torin took the opportunity to kneel in front of her and pull out the jewelry box he had just picked up. Janay looked at him and stopped laughing.

"Janay Constance Williams, I love you and I wanna spend the rest of my life with you. Will you please do me the honor of being my wifey?"

"Oh my god! Are you for real, babe?"

"Yes. I want there to be us. We can work on bettering our lives forever."

"Forever?"

"Forever."

CPSIA information can be obtained at www.ICGtesting.com
Printed in the USA
LVOW10s2121280416

485843LV00014B/183/P